LOOS
THE NIGHTMARE FISH

SEA
QUEST

BY ADAM BLADE

ORCHARD

WAR IS COMING TO THE DELTA
QUADRANT!

For too long I have hidden in
exile, watching as Gustados, the
greatest of all civilisations,
becomes weak.

I have swum amongst the Merryn
of Sumara in disguise as one of
them, and stolen their secrets.
I have walked into Aquora,
Arctiria, Verdula and Gustados,
invisible to any around me. Now I
know how to destroy them.

Deception is the greatest weapon.
With it I will make the so-called
Delta Quadrant Alliance tear
itself apart! And in its place
the Empire of Gustados will rise,
with me as its leader — Kade, the
Lord of Illusion!

CHAPTER ONE

MAX ON ICE

Max lay on the icy shore, shivering as he listened to the breaking waves. Above him he could see nothing but a watery sky full of clouds, scudding along in the wind. Twisting against his bonds, he felt the rough rope chafing against his wrists and ankles.

Max heard a whine coming from his left and turned to see his faithful dogbot, Rivet, lying a few feet away, so tightly wrapped up in coils of rope he looked like a cocoon.

"It won't be for long, boy," Max said. *I hope.*

Max turned his head the other way to see his friend, Lia, standing nearby, inspecting a device on her wrist. "Ready?" he asked, his teeth chattering slightly.

"Cold, Max," Rivet barked.

"This master watch isn't as easy to operate as Cora made it look," Lia said, frowning at the black metal strap on her wrist. Lia wore a black deepsuit, coated in ridges and dotted with tiny nodules. When the suit was turned on, each nodule would project part of a holographic image, disguising the suit's wearer. Their enemy Kade and his minions used the suits. So did Kade's evil ally, Cora Blackheart, the notorious pirate. But it looked strange to see Lia wearing one. Especially as her people, the Merryn, were so mistrustful of technology.

Max watched Lia tap a few buttons on the watch, causing a series of extraordinary holograms to spring up around her. First she became a monkey-like Verdulan, then a tall and beautiful Arctirian, then a sea ghost, almost transparent. Finally Lia hit the right button. She flickered and transformed into a perfect replica of Cora Blackheart herself, complete with her shining, robotic peg leg, tangled black hair and long pirate coat. Max knew it was Lia, but he still gasped in surprise at how lifelike the hologram was.

"How do I look?" Lia asked, twirling around and grinning.

"Horrible," Max said. "Exactly like Cora."

"Perfect," Lia said, before suddenly looking nervous. "Time for the next step in the plan."

"You can do it, Lia," Max said, trying to hide his own doubts. *This has to work!*

Lia took a deep breath and tapped another button on the watch.

"Here goes nothing," Lia said. She turned

a little so Max could see the watch screen too. It flashed a couple of times, then a face appeared on it – one that struck anger into Max's heart. *Kade!* He was pale-skinned, and the right side of his face – from his smooth white temple all the way to his almost lipless mouth – shone with a coating of cracked, silvery metal that looked as if it had been melted onto his skin. A narrow tube ran from one of his wide, flat nostrils, down the side of his face, and disappeared into his neck.

"What do you want, Cora?" Kade said irritably.

Will he see through Lia's disguise? It was a risk, but they had to take it if they were going to find out where Kade's secret base was. All they knew about it so far was its name: the Maze of Illusion.

"Well?" Kade snapped as Lia hesitated. "Are you just going to stare at me?"

Max frowned, anxiously willing Lia on, and she managed to stammer out a response.

"Err. Arr, me hearty," she began, trying to sound like Cora. "Avast…I have caught that…landlubber that's been causing you trouble. And his dog."

"Really?" Kade replied, suddenly looking interested and leaning closer to the camera. Max could see blue veins standing out on his temples. "And the fish-girl?"

"Got away. Arr," Lia replied. "She's quick and clever and brave to boot, not to mention—"

"Show me the captives," Kade barked. Lia turned her wrist to show Max and Rivet lying on the icy ground.

Max wriggled and twisted, trying to make it look convincing. "You'll never get away with this, Cora," he cried.

Rivet whined and barked. "Let Max go."

"Arr, I'll bring them to you," Lia said. "What are your coordinates?"

Kade paused, peering intently at the bound Max and Rivet through the watch screen.

Max held his breath. *This could be our last chance to stop the war.*

Then Kade nodded. "Excellent. 104 – 71 – 134. Get here quickly." With that, the watch screen blinked out and Kade was gone. Max's heart surged and Lia punched the air with joy before rushing over to untie Max's bonds.

"You were brilliant," Max said. He high-fived Lia and they grinned at each other. "We don't have a moment to lose. We need to get to the Maze of Illusion and stop Kade before he causes more trouble between the Delta Quadrant Alliance members."

"Count me in," Lia said grimly. "And don't forget, there's still one temple guardian left to deal with."

Max shuddered. The temple guardians were four ancient sea creatures sacred to the Merryn, but Kade had gained control of them, making them loyal to him. He had also made them even deadlier with the addition of robotic weaponry. Kade controlled them with a ring he'd stolen from Lia's mother. The only way to free the creatures was to remove glowing stones of power from their heads.

"We should get going," said Max. "But first we'd better call my father back in Aquora." Lia nodded and tapped a few more buttons on the watch.

"Hey," Max said with a grin. "Looks like you're finally learning to love technology."

"Only for the Quest," Lia said defensively, as Max's father appeared on the watch screen.

"Max!" cried Callum, his face a mask of relief. "You don't know how good it is to see you alive and well."

"You too, Dad," Max said. He hadn't seen his parents for weeks and was really missing them. But there was no going home yet. *Not until Kade is captured and brought to justice.*

Max gave his father the coordinates of Kade's base. "I'll gather the Aquoran forces and head there straight away," Callum said. "Just one thing, Max. When we mobilise the fleet, we'll run the risk of angering our

allies and starting a war."

"That's a risk we just have to take," Max said. *Anything to stop Kade.*

Callum nodded. "To be completely honest with you, Max, the Gustadians, Arctirians and Verdulans are at each other's throats already. We don't have much time."

"We're closer to the base than you," Max said. "We'll head there immediately."

Callum frowned briefly but then agreed. "I know you can handle yourself, Max. But Kade is a powerful and treacherous enemy. So be careful, understand?"

Max nodded. "Goodbye, Dad. For now."

"I'll see you soon, Max," Callum said, before the screen went blank.

"We should tell my people too," Lia said. "I'll summon Spike." She trotted down the beach to the water's edge. Max saw her bow her head and knew that she was using her Aqua Powers to communicate telepathically.

"Max!" Rivet was still tied up on the ground.

"Sorry, boy," Max said, kneeling to loosen Rivet's bonds. "How could I forget you?"

Lia's swordfish, Spike, had appeared in the shallows. Seeing her, he thrashed in alarm.

"Turn off your hologram!" Max cried. Lia looked down, realising she was still in disguise as Cora Blackheart.

"Sorry, Spike," she said, tapping her wrist and turning back into Lia, before diving into the waves. Max grinned as he watched her rub her pet's belly to reassure him. She murmured to Spike for a couple of minutes, then gave him a hug. The swordfish turned and raced into the depths, heading towards Sumara to pass the message on. When Lia came splashing from the shallows, Max thought she looked downcast. He knew she would miss Spike.

"Come on, Rivet," Max called. "Let's go." He led the way over to where he'd left his aquasphere. He grinned and took a moment to admire the design of the vessel. It could travel both in and out of the water. On land, the aquasphere's outer hull spun like a rolling ball, but the cabin within ran on bearings and so stayed level.

Rivet, Max and Lia climbed into the snug cabin. Max and Lia strapped themselves into the two fixed seats while the dogbot clambered up onto Lia's lap. Max punched the coordinates into the navigation computer. His stomach filled with butterflies as he waited for the computer to locate Kade's base. *Where are you hiding, Kade?*

The map scrolled to the right, coming to a stop over the Barren Ocean, just east of the boundary of the Delta Quadrant. "That's the middle of nowhere," Max muttered. He tapped a few buttons, zooming in, looking for more detail. *And there it is.*

Max saw a tiny circle of rocky islands, right in the middle of the Barren Ocean, roughly in line with Gustados.

"That's it?" Lia asked, sounding unsure.

"It must be," Max said. "There's nothing

else for hundreds of miles around." He powered up the thrusters, feeling the familiar thrum of the roaring engines, his whole body tingling at the thought of the Quest to come. They'd waited long enough. Max gunned the engines and drove the aquasphere into the foaming ocean.

I'm coming for you, Kade.

CHAPTER TWO

RING OF FIRE

Max tapped the temperature gauge and peered at the reading. "We must be getting close," he said. "The water temperature has increased a lot."

Lia sneezed loudly, making Rivet jump in surprise. "Pleased to hear it," she said. "I really didn't enjoy swimming in the freezing seas around Arctiria."

"That's why we Aquorans like to travel inside nice, warm submarines," Max said. "Especially when they have heated seats."

"Hmph," Lia said, blowing her nose. "Give me a warm current in the Sumaran seas anytime."

An alarm pinged on the console and Max's heart surged with excitement. "We're approaching the coordinates," he said. He steered the aquasphere up to the surface, water pouring off its sides as it bobbed up above the waves. Max peered ahead, and saw a ring of small, cone-shaped islands in the distance.

Max took the aquasphere down again to the safety of the ocean depths, racing onwards. He slowed as they approached the undersea mountains whose very tops they'd just seen breaking the surface. Now they were closer, Max could see that each island was in fact connected to the next by a ridge of rock, forming an impenetrable ring. Max guessed the ring of islands was actually the circular cone of an extinct volcano. Lia leaned forward, peering intently ahead.

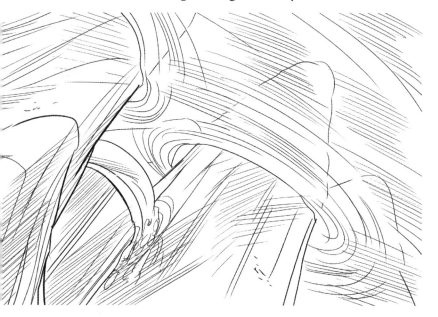

"Wait! I've seen pictures of this place before," Lia exclaimed. "I'm sure of it. I think the old legends mention this volcano."

"What was it used as?" Max asked, intrigued. "A fortress?"

Lia frowned. "I don't remember," she said. "Sorry. I spent most of my history lessons daydreaming about current-surfing."

"Well, do the legends say how to get inside?" Max asked. He took the aquasphere around the volcano, looking for a way in.

"Nope. I think I was sick that day," Lia said. "But, look, there's a break in the ring. Like a gateway."

As they came closer, Max saw that the gateway had an arch over it and a heavy steel door blocking access. It was clear that someone had gone to a lot of trouble to keep visitors out. Max's heart sped up at the thought.

"Rivet, can you use your scanner to see

what's underneath here?" he said.

Rivet's eyes flashed and a second later the dogbot projected the results of the scan onto the aquasphere's monitor. Max gasped. He saw a vast network of straight lines spreading out beneath them, and at its centre a huge cavern, deep under the volcano.

"It's a labyrinth of tunnels," he said. "And so complex! Just like Kade to try to confuse his enemies like this."

"I guess now we know why it's called the Maze of Illusion," Lia said. Max tried to follow the lines with his finger, looking for a path through to the centre, but he quickly lost his way. It didn't help that the image kept flickering and fading.

"Let's get a little closer," he said. "Maybe we'll get a better signal."

But as they moved closer to the side of the undersea mountain, the image faded even more. "The compass is going crazy," Max said, watching the little instrument spin like a top.

Lia pointed at the rocks below. "Look!" she cried. Streaks of some sort of metal ore shone through the dark water. "Maybe that's what's interfering with the instruments."

"Kade chose this location well," Max said. "Looks like you're going to have to pretend to be Cora again. It's the only way Kade will let us in." He opened the aquasphere's dashboard and took out three large, coloured gemstones.

Lia swallowed nervously. "Are you sure, Max? It means giving ourselves up without a fight."

"I can't see another way," Max replied. "But as long as we're prepared, there's every chance this plan might work. First we need to keep these stones somewhere safe." Max opened Rivet's back storage compartment and placed the stones inside. *I'm not about to let them fall back into Kade's hands.*

Max shivered as he remembered that there was still one stone unrecovered, and one terrifying guardian out there, under Kade's control. He looked at Lia and nodded. "Let's do this," he said.

Lia tapped a few buttons on her watch, and became Cora once again. "How do I look?" she asked.

"Even more horrible than before, if possible," Max said, trying to make light of the situation. Lia could only manage a brief smile.

They each slipped a tiny communicator device into their ears to ensure they could talk to each other when in the water. Max tucked a blaster inside his deepsuit and gave his hyperblade to Lia to carry. He suspected Kade would be watching as they approached, so he couldn't be seen carrying a weapon. Then the three of them left the aquasphere through the airlock and swam slowly towards the steel doors, every moment wondering if Kade might send one of his twisted robo-creatures to attack them.

Max felt he should say something encouraging, but there was a lump in his throat, and just thinking about what they were trying to do made his stomach churn.

As they approached the massive steel doors, Max noticed a camera swivelling to track them and pointed it out to Lia. She stopped and cried out in her best pirate voice. "Aha… Arr there, me hearty. I have your captives here. Like you said. Now open up, you filthy landlubber." She poked Max lightly with the point of the hyperblade.

"Ow," Max whispered through the communicator. "Easy!"

"Sorry, but I have to make it seem convincing," Lia replied.

Her performance seemed to have done the trick, because Max heard a great rumbling sound deep within the rocks and saw a chink of light appear at one side of the door as it slid open. As soon the gap was wide enough, Max swam inside, blinking against the bright light. Lia and Rivet followed. Max looked around, and saw they were in a rocky passageway wide enough to take in an Aquoran battle sub. The walls were streaked with the strange dark metal Max had seen from the aquasphere. But the strangest sight of all was the source of the bright light itself. It came from thousands and thousands of glowing anemones lining the walls, their shining tentacles waving gently in the current, sending warm, rippling light throughout the chamber.

"They've been robotically altered," Lia said, inspecting one of the strange creatures. Max swam over to see that Lia was right; circuitry was visible through the glowing skin of the anemone. "They're half a living creature, and half a wall light." Max turned at the sound of the door grinding shut behind them. *There's no going back now.*

"Max," Lia said, with panic in her voice. He turned back to her, and it took him a second to realise what was wrong. Lia no longer looked like Cora. She was her usual Merryn self. "The disguise, it just blinked out." She tapped the watch again

frantically, but nothing happened.

Max's heart sank. *Exposed so soon! Why had I ever thought this might work?* Just then, an intercom crackled from somewhere close by and Max heard a voice he knew all too well.

"Welcome to the Maze of Illusion," Kade said, a note of triumph in his voice. "Did you really think I would be fooled by one of my own devices?"

"Show yourself," Max cried. "Let's end this now. In single combat."

"And miss out on all the fun?" Kade replied. "I've been waiting too long for that. You still have no idea what you've got yourself into. The Maze of Illusion is the most fiendish test of skill, bravery and intelligence ever invented. It was built thousands of years ago, to test young Merryn warriors."

Max turned to Lia, who looked embarrassed.

"Oh, that's right," she said. "Now I remember."

Kade went on. "The rocks are magnetic, so compasses will not work. The maze is so vast that no one can possibly remember it all, and no maps exist. Only the very bravest, strongest and cleverest Merryn ever made it to the centre. Most were lost, or killed by booby traps."

"And you are in the centre?" Max asked. He knew he needed to get as much information from Kade as possible.

"Oh, yes," Kade said. "I made it here, though it was far from easy, even for me. You have no chance, even with your robot mutt and the fish-girl."

"The three of us certainly put up a fight when we destroyed your base near Gustados," Max said. Maybe if he taunted Kade, his opponent might slip up and reveal something useful.

There was a brief pause. "You did set me back, I must admit," Kade replied slowly, as if trying to keep his temper in check. "But I have many supporters in Gustados. They will soon help me usurp the coward General Phero. When the inevitable war begins, the Gustadians will know who to turn to."

"Who?" Max asked. "A clown fish?"

"If you think insults will save your life, you are much mistaken," Kade said quietly. "I will lead the Gustadian Empire to victory over all of the Delta Quadrant. Your bones will lie at the bottom of the ocean, picked clean by sea creatures." The buzz of the intercom died and Max, Lia and Rivet were left in silence.

"What now?" Lia asked, handing Max his hyperblade. She looked around nervously, as if expecting an attack from Kade's minions at any moment.

"There's not much choice," Max said,

looking down the long passageway ahead. It sloped down after a hundred yards or so, dropping out of sight. Max sheathed the hyperblade and led the three of them forward, alert for the faintest sign of movement.

Away from the main entrance, he saw the glowing anemones thinned out a little. Their light wasn't quite able to completely pierce the murky water, and shadows seemed to lie in wait for Max and Lia, only to be revealed as rocks or an uneven floor. After they'd travelled for a few minutes, Max saw through the gloom that the passageway split into a three-way fork.

"Which way, Max?" Rivet barked.

Max frowned, trying to remember the map he'd seen back in the aquasphere. It was definitely not straight on, he knew that. *So is it right or left?*

"Can you remember which way it was?"

Lia asked. "I think it was left first, then a right, but after that…"

Max closed his eyes and tried to visualise the layout of the maze that he'd seen projected from Rivet's scanner. *No good.* He made a decision and took them down the left-hand fork.

But only twenty yards into the side tunnel, they came to a dead end.

"That's odd," Lia said. "I must have remembered wrong."

"No, I remembered it the same way," Max replied. They were just about to turn to head back when he noticed something. The wall… had it just moved? He swam towards the rugged rock face to inspect it more closely, when suddenly the entire wall seemed to shift and tumble. Max sprang back in alarm, his heart pounding as the rocks broke up and surged towards him. He shouted out a

warning as he realised what was happening.
It's a false wall! Max saw a dozen Gustadian
minions wearing holo-suits, disguised as the
very rocks themselves.

They pointed their blasters at Max, and
squeezed the triggers.

CHAPTER THREE

WALL OF FEAR

"Down, Max!" barked Rivet.

Max ducked quickly as the dogbot shot overhead, smashing into the cluster of Gustadian minions and sending them flying. Max felt one of the energy bolts sear his hand as he bashed against the rocky floor. A second bolt glanced off Rivet's tough steel flank but the others went wide. Max spun to make sure Lia hadn't been hit and was relieved to see she had dived for cover behind a rock spur in the side wall.

Max pulled out his blaster, and before the minions could reassemble themselves he fired off a fusillade of shots. The Gustadians scattered for cover as Rivet turned back and raced towards Max.

"Quick," Max cried. "Go!" He saw Lia fly back up the passageway, Rivet just behind. Max fired off a few more shots to keep the Gustadians pinned down, then turned to follow his friends. After a few seconds he heard the minions returning fire; blaster shots sizzling past him. Max's hand stung from the glancing blow he'd received, but the damage wasn't too bad. They swam quickly to get around the curving wall of the tunnel, putting solid rock between themselves and the pursuers.

When they reached the place where the tunnel forked, Max turned and raised his blaster. "Get back," he called, and fired

three times into the roof of the left-hand fork, a dozen yards inside the tunnel. Max watched with satisfaction as, with a crack and a tremendous rumbling sound, the roof collapsed and sent hundreds of tons of rock tumbling down, blocking the tunnel completely.

Max heard Lia sneezing as the dust cleared, and beyond the blockage he heard the faint shouts of the Gustadians he'd trapped. "They sound angry," he said.

"Come, Max!" Rivet barked impatiently.

The dogbot led them down the right-hand tunnel. This time Max watched the walls very carefully. Rivet used his snout lamp to help light the way. As the tunnel grew darker, Max felt the cold clutch of fear grip him more tightly. There was something about this place that filled him with despair. Apart from the sparse anemones, there was little sign of life – just a few scuttling black crabs Max was careful to avoid. They seemed to have strong, sharp claws.

Max tried not to think about what else might be hiding in the darkness. Instead, he concentrated hard on remembering the route. Every hundred yards or so they came to a fork in the passage and he had to decide which way to go. Luckily, Lia also remembered some of the map, and on the few occasions when Max really had no idea which way to go, Lia came up with the answer...or an answer, at least.

"It's not just a question of remembering the rights and lefts," Lia said, when they'd got to a particularly confusing junction. "It's the ups and downs as well. Which way do you think? Right, left, forward, up or down?"

"You forgot one," Max said. "We could turn around and go back. We can't be entirely sure we've even come the right way."

"It's forward," Lia said. "I'm sure of it. The other passages are just here to confuse us."

"Well, it's working," Max said with a sigh. The further they travelled into the maze, the less sure of himself he was.

To make matters worse, the anemones had

disappeared all together, and they were left with Rivet's snout lamp, which only pierced the dark a dozen yards ahead. On and on they went, seeing nothing but the dim surface of the floor a few feet before them, when suddenly Lia yelped in alarm, sending Max's heart racing. "What is it?" he said, raising his blaster, finger twitching on the trigger.

"There," Lia said, pointing. Peering ahead, Max saw something white lying on the floor of the tunnel. *A skeleton!*

Max moved closer. The skeleton's clothes were tattered rags, but around its neck still hung a necklace of shark teeth. Clutched in one hand Max saw a thin sword.

"It's Merryn," Lia said. "Male."

"He must have been looking for the centre of the maze," Max said. "But he never made it."

Lia knelt beside the skeleton. "Rest in

peace," she said.

"Light, Max," Rivet barked, looking down the dark passage.

Max looked up to see there was indeed a red light visible in the distance. "More anemones?" he asked.

"Those aren't red," Lia pointed out.

"Maybe it's a door?"

"There's only one way to find out," Max said firmly. He pushed off and swam steadily down the passage, with the others close behind.

As they approached, the red glow throbbed, shifting colours. "It almost looks organic," Max said, filled with wonder at the haunting light which melted the darkness away.

"Max," Lia called out softly behind him. But he was close now, almost close enough to touch the light. He could see it was rounded in shape, about the size of his head. It changed colour again, glowing a calm, welcoming pink. He stretched out a hand and kicked his legs, gliding closer and closer…

"Max!" Lia cried more urgently. But her voice sounded far away.

Later, Lia. Just let me get a little closer…

It was so soft and comforting, after all the

cold darkness of the maze. Max reached out, but just as he was about to touch the glowing light, it moved quickly to one side to reveal something immediately behind it.

A huge, terrifying face.

Max darted backwards, shocked out of his trance. His heart was racing. This wasn't just any face. Behind the light lurked a giant fish, monstrously large, and as Max dodged away it opened its huge jaws to reveal a crowded set of teeth, long and cruel. *It's a temple guardian!*

"Max!" Lia screamed. Somewhere he heard Rivet barking, too far away to save him this time. And he heard something else too – the crackling of an intercom system, and Kade's sinister voice.

"I see you've found my pet," Kade said. "I call it Loosejaw, the Nightmare Fish. Now prepare to die."

CHAPTER FOUR

THE JAWS OF DEFEAT

Terror struck Max as the huge fish lunged forward and shut its jaws around him, one of the teeth gashing his arm. The pain stung him into action. Inside the beast's throat, he saw something extraordinary. Its mouth had no base. The lower jaw was just a hinged bone with jagged teeth embedded in it. Max could see the dim, flickering light of Rivet's snout lamp through the gap. *I guess that's why it's called Loosejaw!*

Max felt his body pulled towards the fish's gullet as it prepared to swallow him whole. But he lashed out with both feet, jamming himself against the lower jaw and dislodging a couple of teeth. Then he dived down and slipped out through the gap. One of the creature's long, jagged teeth came floating down alongside him, and instinctively he snatched at it and shoved it into his pocket.

There was no time to rest. He was still perilously close to a giant fish with razor-sharp teeth. And they weren't the only weapons the creature had. Max saw a snub-nosed torpedo sitting in a tube strapped to the Robobeast's flank. There were more stored in a rack, feeding an automatic delivery system. *There's no way of outrunning those.*

Loosejaw turned to snap at him, and Max

ducked behind the fish, grabbing its tail. The water swirled as the fish twisted and thrashed, trying to throw him off. Max grunted with the effort, feeling the enormous power of the tail whipping him back and forth, slamming him against the walls of the tunnel.

Max heard Rivet barking and realised his dogbot was trying to distract Loosejaw. It worked! The giant fish dived straight for Rivet, who had appeared in the dim light ahead, dragging Max along with it.

"Swim!" Max shouted. Rivet spun and darted back down the tunnel in a flash. Max saw Lia next, her eyes widening in alarm as the creature headed in her direction.

"Grab on, Lia," Rivet barked. Lia wrapped her arms around the dogbot's neck and he raced off, tail propeller whirring. The fish went after them like a rocket, Max gripping tightly to its tail fin.

Max crawled forwards, dragging himself against the slipstream, up the fish's back until he was clinging to the dorsal fin. He knew his bulk would be slowing the fish down a little; even so, Loosejaw was gaining on Rivet and Lia. Rivet's nose beam swept back and forth in the darkness. The fish's red light glowed ominously, flashing slowly in a regular pattern, lighting up Max's friends from behind. It was an eerie sight. Max held on desperately. If he came off at this speed, he'd be cut to ribbons against the wall's sharp rocks.

He edged forwards a little more and peered at the red light. It was coming from a stone, embedded between the creature's eyes. If only Max could prise the jewel from its forehead…
But before he could move again, he saw the pattern of the red light had changed. Now it was steady. He watched as the light formed itself into a narrow cone that sought out Lia

before locking on to her and pulsing sharply.

Max gasped as Lia went limp. Letting go of the dogbot, she dropped to the tunnel floor. The light then locked onto Rivet and, after a series of pulses, Rivet too froze and stopped. He tumbled lazily in the dark water before coming to rest against a rock wall. Max's heart

hammered in his chest. *They're helpless!*

Loosejaw slowed as it reached the floating Lia and opened its jaws wider than ever.

Max stood up on the creature's back and drew his hyperblade. He raised it high and brought it slashing down onto the creature's head, aiming for the stone. He missed, and the blade sank deep into the creature's flesh. The light blinked out, and Loosejaw erupted in a frenzy of thrashing, throwing Max to one side, the hyperblade torn from his grip.

To his relief, Max saw that Lia and Rivet had started moving again. Lia grabbed hold of Rivet once more and pointed upwards. A moment later she and Rivet shot up into a narrow vertical passage above. Max raced after them and made it to the tunnel opening before remembering his weapon. *I can't lose the hyperblade. If I do we'll be defenceless!* He turned back to look, and found himself face to face with Loosejaw, the red light glowing again. His heart leapt in fear.

He started to reach for his blaster, but something made him stop. Just as quickly as the panic had hit him, it was gone. Instead he felt comforted as the beautiful red light washed over him, bathing him in its warmth. He relaxed. *Why move? Why fight any more?* The great jaws opened, and the gaping maw came closer, enveloping him…

With a jerk, Max felt himself hauled back and upwards. In a daze, he saw Lia looking at him. She'd rescued him with her spear.

"Honestly, will you stop looking at the red light?" she said impatiently.

"Thanks," Max said, shaking his head to clear it. He looked down to see Loosejaw swimming back and forth, glaring up at them. The passage was far too small for it to follow. Then the creature stopped and positioned itself right below the opening, pointing its body up at them. Max remembered what he'd seen strapped to its side earlier.

"Torpedoes!" Max yelled. "Move!"

The three of them darted away, this time directly up the chimney. Max heard a whining sound behind them as Loosejaw armed its deadly weapon. "Faster," he panted. Then there was a *click* and a *hiss*: the sounds of a torpedo being released into the water. Then two more. *CLICK, hiss, CLICK, hiss.*

"Grab Rivet's legs," Max cried. Lia didn't need to be told twice; she and Max each took a firm grip on the dogbot and Rivet powered them effortlessly up the vertical passage.

BOOM! The tunnel rocked with an explosion beneath. The shockwave gripped Max and smashed him hard against the side of the narrow chimney before driving them onwards and upwards. *We're out of control!*

Max felt the rough stone raking his back and heard Lia yelp with pain as she too was battered against the walls.

"Faster," Max cried. "I see a side tunnel up ahead! We can shelter in there."

Rivet redoubled his efforts as a second explosion went off. Max felt another hard kick in the guts. Lia screamed as she was jammed against the rocks. Her grip on Rivet's legs was slipping.

"Max!" she cried. He reached out a hand… but too late. Lia lost her hold and fell behind as Rivet carried on powering up the chimney.

The dogbot darted into the side tunnel where Max released his grasp.

"We have to go back for Lia!" Max cried.

Rivet spun and shot back the way they'd come, Max following. Before they got more than a few feet, the tunnel was rocked by a massive explosion as the third torpedo

exploded right below them.

Max's breath was knocked out of him as he was hurled down the narrow side tunnel by the shockwave, Rivet tumbling beside him.

The torpedo had exploded in the vertical shaft...right where Lia had been.

CHAPTER FIVE

BURIED, ALIVE?

Slumped in the darkness, Max lay dazed and defeated. His head ached. Could Lia really be gone? *It can't end like this!*

Rivet freed himself from some loose rocks that had fallen on him and swam over to Max, nuzzling his master. "Up, Max!" Rivet barked.

Max forced himself upright. Behind him an avalanche of rock blocked the way into the vertical tunnel they had come up. *I can't give up on Lia,* he thought. Max scooted to the fallen rocks and shouted as loudly as he could. "Lia! Lia!" He began to hurl away the rocks. He wouldn't stop until he got her out.

"Yes, Max! Dig!" Rivet darted forwards and started to burrow into the mound of fallen rocks, grinding them up with his great jaws and kicking the rubble behind with his paws. Max ducked under a piece of flying rock and retreated a few feet to give Rivet space to work. The side tunnel carried on, sloping downwards, and Max peered into the gloom. *Is that a dim light?* Max didn't want to stray far from where Lia might still be imprisoned, but he swam a short distance along, to check for danger, struck by the thought that Loosejaw could be coming up behind them. Then, as the sound of Rivet's digging receded, he thought he heard another sound. *A voice!*

"Max! It's Lia, I need your help!"

Max's heart pounded. "Lia, where are you?" he called. He shook his head, trying to clear the fog from his brain. Which way had the voice come from? Was his mind playing tricks on him? How was it possible that Lia had managed to get ahead of them? *Maybe Loosejaw's torpedo blew open another tunnel.* Hope flared in his chest. He grinned. *Trust Lia to be one step ahead.* He swam on more quickly down the tunnel.

"I'm hurt," Lia's voice cried out, loud and clear. She sounded in pain. "One of Kade's soldiers got me."

Max squinted again, peering down the tunnel towards the light. A figure was lying under a cluster of glowing anemones.

"Max!" the figure cried.

"Lia!" Max darted down the passageway to where she lay on the floor, face down. "How did you get here?" He turned to shout back up the tunnel. "Riv, I've found her!" As he knelt by his friend, she suddenly whipped an arm around and Max felt a sharp crack on his jaw. He lurched back and hit the rock wall with a thud, the breath knocked out of him.

Lia stood and held a blaster, pointed right at him. Max gasped. Had she gone mad? Her lip curled and she squeezed the trigger.

Max darted forwards and knocked the blaster aside just as Lia fired. He felt the impact behind him as the blaster's energy

bolt slammed into the wall of the passage, dislodging rocks, which came tumbling down around them. One hit Lia on the shoulder. Max started back as he saw the tell-tale flicker of a hologram. *Of course!* It wasn't Lia at all, but one of Kade's henchmen in a holo-suit. The minion went to level the blaster at Max again, but Max lashed out with his foot and knocked the weapon from his enemy's fingers. It skittered down the passageway.

Max tried to reach *his* blaster, but the Gustadian roared, seized Max in an iron grip and threw him to the floor. Max stretched up, trying to shove his attacker's face away, but he could do nothing to stop the minion from picking up one of the heavy rocks that had fallen from the roof. Max's chest tightened as the Gustadian lifted the sharp rock high.

The fake Lia snarled and brought the rock down, aiming right at Max's head.

CHAPTER SIX

SEEING DOUBLE!

As the rock came down hard, Max twisted his head and felt the sharp edge scrape his temple. Pain exploded in his head and adrenaline and anger surged through him. *I won't let the Quest end here, not like this!*

Max reached down deep within himself, and somehow found the strength for a powerful shove against his enemy's chest. Surprised, the Gustadian fell backwards and Max kicked his legs up to throw his unbalanced attacker off to the side. The fake

Lia kicked hard down the passage, going after the blaster.

Quick as an eel, Max righted himself and drew his own blaster, just as his enemy grabbed his, turned and aimed.

They fired at the same time, but only Max's aim was true. The minion was thrown backwards by the stun bolt and hit the wall, before sliding down onto the floor, unconscious.

Max bent his knees and slid gently downwards, exhausted. His head hurt from where the rock had hit. His back still stung from being scraped along the wall. He wanted to lie down and sleep, but a movement down the tunnel caught his eye.

"Lia?" he asked cautiously. The Merryn girl floated in the passageway, staring down at her double in astonishment. Behind her Max saw Rivet, looking every bit as confused.

"Two Lias, Max!" Rivet barked.

"Max," Lia cried, when she saw him slumped on the rocks. She stepped towards him.

Max held up a hand. "Wait! How can I tell you are really Lia?" he said uncertainly. His head was still swimming, but he wouldn't be fooled again.

"Of course it's me! I heard the blaster fire and followed it."

"Wait, wait," he replied, trying to think. He shook his head to clear it. "I know. I'll ask you something only the real Lia would know. What is my favourite band?"

"Max," Lia sighed, rolling her eyes. "We don't have time for a pop quiz."

"Please," Max said, hoping desperately that Lia would be able to give him the right answer. "Just tell me, who is my favourite band?"

Lia sighed again. "The Psychotic Sharks, of course. But I have no idea why."

Max smiled and lowered his hand. "They're awesome, that's why."

"Are you OK?" Lia asked, coming closer and peering at his forehead.

Max lifted a hand to his temple and could feel the sting of the cut where the Gustadian had hit him with the rock. "I'll live," Max said. Now he had his friends with him, he could feel the strength returning to his muscles. He rose to his feet. "Come on. We have a Quest to complete."

Max, Lia and Rivet carried on down the passageway. Bright light shone from a corner up ahead. As they got closer, Max realised it was coming from the entranceway to a great cavern. The three friends peered cautiously inside. It took a while for Max's eyes to adjust, then he gasped at what he saw.

The chamber was vast, reaching so far up it could have fit twenty aquaspheres, stacked on top of one another. Almost every centimetre of the great cavern's walls was occupied by a brightly glowing anemone.

"That's why the light is so bright," Max said in a hushed tone. "There must be millions of anemones."

He crouched by the entranceway, looking for movement or other signs of life. But the chamber seemed empty. Empty, except for a large glass dome, as big as a battle sub, right in the centre of the rocky floor. *I need to see what's inside.*

Max swallowed and swam out across the cavern floor, feeling very exposed. He turned briefly to see that Lia and Rivet were following. He reached the dome and used his hand to shield against the glare, peering within. Inside the dome he saw a strange mix

of objects: ancient weapons, axes, swords and bows and arrows hung around the walls. *Like a museum of warfare.* But there was a sleek aquabike of modern design too, and in the far corner a rack of holo-suits. Max could also see a long computer console with monitors, a keyboard and a range of instruments and buttons whose function he

could only guess at. But strangest of all was a piece of equipment right in the middle of the dome space – a tall, cylindrical machine with an array of signal dishes, like one of the comm towers back on Aquora.

"What is it?" Lia asked, reaching out a hand to touch the glass of the dome. "A receiver?"

"I think it's the opposite," Max replied. "I

think it's a transmitter."

"Transmitting what?" Lia asked.

"Could be anything," Max replied. "But at the moment I'm guessing it's transmitting a jamming signal. I think this is the device Kade has been using to block transmissions within the quadrant."

"Max, watch out!" Rivet suddenly barked. Max spun quickly, and his heart lurched as he saw what Rivet had spotted. *Loosejaw!* Except this time there was a figure riding on its back. Clad in close-fitting black armour, Kade wore a manic grin on his pale, blue-veined face. *They're coming right for us!*

Max was about to tell the others to escape, when the red stone on Loosejaw's forehead suddenly lit up and shone right at him. Suddenly he felt his willpower draining away and his movement slowing.

"Max!" Lia cried. "Don't look!" But he

couldn't stop himself.

What was he about to do? Escape? But why? The light was so beautiful.

He floated, entranced, and watched his enemies approach. From what seemed a long way away, he heard Kade's triumphant voice.

"I have you now, Max. I have you now."

CHAPTER SEVEN

ALL TIED UP AGAIN

Max woke to find his arms twisted and bound uncomfortably behind him. He heard a deep humming noise and felt the vibrations of some piece of machinery at his back. He tried to turn, but he couldn't. *What am I tied to?*

"Max, are you awake?" Lia hissed from behind him.

"Where are we?" Max asked, looking around blearily. He saw Rivet lying a few feet away, tied up with thick rope again like he had been on the frozen shore. But this time it was for real. Rivet looked up at him and whined.

"We're tied to that transmitter thing inside the glass dome," Lia said.

Max took a few breaths, only just now realising that he was breathing air, not

water. He was so used to a life underwater now that sometimes he could hardly tell the difference. "I don't remember anything," he said, searching his memory.

"No, you were completely out of it," Lia said. "Rivet and I were a bit dazed, but you completely froze up again, as soon as you saw the red light."

As she spoke, Max caught a glimpse of the giant form of Loosejaw swimming by outside the dome, as if it were patrolling, guarding them. *Where is Kade?* He twisted and pulled at the bonds that held them both, wondering if he could fray them until they snapped.

"Max," Lia said. "If we escape from this, will you promise me one thing?"

"Of course. What?"

"Promise me that you'll stop looking at Loosejaw's stupid red light."

"I promise," Max said, grinning despite

the situation. He rubbed the rope against the rough metal of the transmitter.

"That won't work, I'm afraid," Kade said, suddenly stepping out in front of Max. Lit from behind by the great wall of anemones, his twisted face was in shadow. "They're Gustadian coil ropes. Unbreakable."

We'll see about that, Max thought. His fingers felt a lump in his back pocket. *Loosejaw's tooth.* He knew there had been a reason he'd grabbed it back in the tunnel. With Kade standing right before him, his hands were hidden from view, and Max eased it out of his pocket and began sawing at the rope with the serrated edge. With luck, the drone of the machine would drown out the sawing sound.

"Now, tell me where the stones are," Kade said. "I'd rather like my guardians back."

"What stones?" Max asked innocently.

"Come on," Kade said irritably. "Don't play

games with me."

"Honestly," Max said, sounding a lot more confident than he felt. "I don't know what you're talking about. Do you know anything about some stones, Lia?"

"I never saw any stones," Lia said.

Kade strode towards them and Max was suddenly struck with fear at the thought that Kade had noticed him sawing away and was about to take the tooth. But, instead, the Gustadian pulled his blaster and pointed it at Lia's temple. The ring he'd stolen from Sumara gleamed on his finger.

"Give that back!" shouted Lia. "That belonged to my mother."

Kade ignored her. "You have three seconds to tell me where the stones are," he said coolly.

Max swallowed. He couldn't let Kade have the stones. With four temple guardians under his control again, he would be unstoppable.

"Three…" Kade said. "Two…"

Max sawed furiously. The Gustadian rope was strong, and he needed to break it fast.

"One!"

"Wait, wait," Lia cried. "I have something to tell you."

"Just in time," Kade said, laughing cruelly. "Though I thought Max here might give in first. Maybe he doesn't care as much about you as you imagined."

"Are you going to listen to what I have to say," Lia asked, "or just stand there gloating?"

"Please carry on," Kade said in a mocking tone. "I do apologise."

"I think," Lia began, "that you should turn on your vid-screen and see what's just arrived at your gates."

"What are you talking about?" Kade demanded. But he did as Lia suggested.

As the screen flickered into life, Max gasped in amazement at what he saw. Filling the screen, stretching back into the murky depths outside the base, waited rank upon rank of Merryn warriors riding armoured swordfish and orcas. He even saw some humpback whales, loaded with spear-wielding warriors.

His heart surged with hope and he heard Lia laugh with pride as she twisted her head to see the screen.

"My people are here," she said. "What's more, the Aquoran forces are minutes away."

"You can't know that," Kade said. "All signals are blocked."

Max noticed that the Gustadian didn't seem at all alarmed by the news. The thought worried him.

"If you wanted to block all signals," Lia said, "then tying us to a transmitter was a big mistake. I can use my Aqua Powers here. I've been communicating with my people for the last half-hour."

Kade let out a bark of laughter. "You shouldn't have told me that," he said, twisting a few dials. "I'll just change the settings and stop you from sending any more messages. Now only I will control what is being broadcast."

But as he spoke, Max saw the Aquoran battle fleet arriving on the vid-screen too. Dozens, no, hundreds, of subs of all sizes, bristling with weaponry. "It's too late," Max said triumphantly. "You'll never escape now the Aquoran fleet is here. Surrender peacefully and we can avoid any more bloodshed."

"Avoiding bloodshed is the last thing on my mind," Kade said. "And you two fools have given me the perfect opportunity to put the final piece of my plan into place."

"What do you mean?" Lia asked, doubt creeping into her voice.

"I had planned to wait before transmitting this," Kade said, crossing to the controls. "But now seems like the perfect time."

Max watched the keyboard carefully as Kade typed. *Now I have his password!*

The image on the screen suddenly changed, to a recording of Max fighting someone in a tunnel. Dread settled in Max's stomach as he saw the figure he was fighting was the Gustadian minion. *The one disguised as Lia!* As he watched himself shoot the fake Lia, the realisation of what Kade was planning froze him to the core. This was being broadcast, through the transmitter, to the Merryn forces

outside the gates. It would seem to them that he'd attacked and killed Lia, and they would believe that the sudden loss of contact with her was because she was dead!

Frantically, he sawed harder at his bonds. *I must stop this!* Then he turned back to look at the screen and saw, with mounting horror, the massed ranks of the Sumaran army turn as one and open fire on the approaching Aquoran battle fleet. After a brief pause, the Aquorans fired back. Max cried out as he saw two X500 class subs hit, then go spiralling down to crash hard into the side of the volcano. A powerful laser blast from a battle sub cut through a battalion of Merryn, sending them tumbling and screaming down, down into the depths.

"No!" Lia shouted.

Max could feel he was nearly through the rope. *I have one chance, and one chance*

only. He glanced back at his friend, who had noticed now how he was sawing at the rope. She looked up and nodded. Max was sure she would know what to do.

Kade turned up the volume and the sound of a chaotic, violent battle outside rang through the chamber. Max tried to block out the screams and explosions and the sickening crunch of whalebone against steel. The whole time Kade laughed and laughed, maniacally. Rivet barked furiously, fighting to escape from his bonds.

With a final wrench at the fraying cord, Max felt the bonds fall loose. Lia was free in a flash and rushed to the nearest wall, where she grabbed an antique Merryn spear. Max ran the opposite way, directly towards the transmitter controls. Kade saw him and pulled his blaster to fire. But Lia hurled the spear, knocking the weapon from the Gustadian's grasp. Max felt his heart swell with pride as his friend seized another weapon, this time a huge battle axe, so big she could hardly lift it. Lia screamed out a war cry and rushed at Kade.

Unarmed, Kade snarled and quickly slapped the master watch he wore on his wrist. He blinked out of sight. Lia stumbled through the suddenly empty space and crashed hard into the wall, the axe clattering to the floor. The next moment Kade reappeared on the other side of the dome and stooped to collect his blaster.

Lia's won me some time! Max turned to the controls, quickly tapping in Kade's password. Then he cut the recording of his fight with the fake Lia and set the transmitter to show what was currently happening in the dome. *Just one last thing…* Accessing the settings, Max changed the password so that Kade couldn't access his own system any more.

"Step away from there!" growled Kade. He strode over to the controls, pointing the blaster. Max raised his hands and backed away from the controls. Kade tapped at the keyboard, then spat with frustration when he realised what Max had done.

"It's over, Kade," Max said. "You might as well give yourself up without a fight. My father will put you in a comfortable prison cell. Your minions can't defeat the Aquoran battle fleet. If you don't surrender they will destroy you and your base too." Out of the corner of his eye he saw Lia had untied Rivet, who was staring fiercely at their enemy.

Kade glared at Max with his one visible eye, cold and blue. The other eye was covered by his black helmet. Max couldn't help but shiver as he looked back at the pale Gustadian. The array of dangerous weaponry, the veined

skin, the thin breathing tube snaking its way out from a hole in his neck and up into his nose…

Kade laughed again. "It doesn't matter now," he said. He flicked a switch, bringing the image on the screen back to the battle outside. Max's stomach flipped in horror as he saw one of the humpback whales ram a 3000-class battle sub amidships, leaving it bent and crumpled. It began to sink slowly. Max hoped the crew would be able to escape, but it was soon lost from view. Individual Merryn warriors on sea creatures were engaged in hand-to-hand combat against deepsuit-wearing Aquorans. A blizzard of blaster shots flashed back and forth, bringing brave troops down again and again.

"What have you done?" Max said despairingly.

"I gave them what they wanted!" Kade cried, stepping closer to Max and hissing. "They have desired this war for years. Even before I set off that bomb. Different races can't get on with each other, Max. The alliance was always doomed to fail."

"You're wrong!" Lia cried. "And you're nothing but a common jewellery thief. Give me back my mother's ring!" She rushed at Kade a second time. Rivet followed, barking angrily. But, once more, with a slap of the wrist, Kade blinked out of view and reappeared on the other side of the dome. Lia slid on the polished floor and crashed against the console.

"Oh, I do like you, fish-girl," Kade said. "You're such fun!" He stepped forward and then looked down as his foot bumped against something. It was the axe Lia had dropped earlier. Kade picked it up and inspected it with a grin. "These weapons are from thousands of years ago, you see. Every race on Nemos has a long history of warfare and bloodshed. You should study your own history, Max. You'd soon realise that I'm right. We just aren't built to be friends."

Rivet barked furiously and raced towards Kade, leaping up at him. But the Gustadian was ready. He stood his ground and swung the huge axe, striking Rivet with a solid blow. The dogbot went sailing across the dome and landed with a sickening thud against the transmitter. There he lay still, a huge dent in his side.

"Rivet!" Max shouted. *I can't lose him!* He fell to his knees beside the robot dog and inspected the damage, hoping he could be repaired. Lia's battle cry rang out once more and he looked up to see her charging at Kade for a third time.

"No," Max called. But it was too late. Kade swung the axe once more. Lia tried to duck and roll underneath the blade, but the axe shaft struck her with a glancing blow across the temple, and Max froze as he watched her slump to the ground, senseless.

"My work here is done," Kade said triumphantly. "You have an irritating habit of interfering with my plans. And since my Robobeast is occupied, I suppose I'll have to take care of you myself, once and for all." And with that, he lifted the axe high above his head, ready to bring down on the unconscious Lia.

CHAPTER EIGHT

LAST CHANCE

Max leaped up onto the control panel, using that to launch himself at Kade. The Gustadian went down, the axe ringing out as it hit the hard floor. But Kade was quickly back on his feet, and by the time Max himself had regained his footing, the Gustadian was already swinging the axe in a low, murderous arc towards him. Max jumped up, pulling his feet high as the blade swished beneath.

Max realised he still held Loosejaw's tooth

in his hand and brandished it at Kade. His opponent simply laughed.

"That's your weapon? A fish tooth?" He swung the axe again and Max parried the blow with the tooth. Incredibly, it survived the impact, though the force juddered agonisingly through Max's arm. Max backed away, forcing Kade to come after him.

"How can you do this, Kade?" Max said, trying to buy time. "How could you put so many lives in danger? How could you blow up innocent civilians at the peace conference?"

Kade shrugged. "Power is everything, Max," he said and swung the axe again. Max blocked the swing once more. Another wave of pain swept up his aching arm. "People are expendable. I'd blow up the whole of Sumara if I had to."

"What's next?" Max asked, backing away again. "Once all the other alliance members

have fought each other into the ground?"

"I lead Gustadian forces into the fray," Kade said, stalking towards him with a wicked grin. "Mop up what's left of the pulverised armies and rule the whole of the Delta Quadrant. A simple plan I expect even you could have guessed."

"No one could guess just how evil you are,"

Max said quietly. Kade sneered and took another swing with the axe, this time even harder. Max parried again with the tooth. He winced as the axe blade smashed into it, shattering it to pieces. He fell to the ground in pain and shock, dimly aware of Kade lifting the axe up again to finish him off.

Max closed his eyes tight and waited for the blow. *I'm sorry, Lia. Sorry, Rivet, Mum and Dad. I'm sorry I wasn't able to complete the most important Quest of all.*

But the blow never came. Max opened his eyes cautiously to see Kade's attention was fixed on the screen. Max sat up and peered, and at once his heart surged with hope. What was left of the Aquoran battle fleet had stopped fighting the Merryn and had brought all its firepower to bear on the gateway instead. The fleet was steadily battering the steel doors and the rocks around it with blasters, lasers and rockets. Max heard rumbling and felt the vibrations as thousands of tons of steel and rock were pulverised under the intense bombardment.

Behind the Aquoran subs the Merryn were waiting, ready to dive into the tunnels as soon as the massive guns stopped. *They're coming! The alliance is alive and they're coming!*

Max saw Kade stride over to the transmitter and inspect it. He looked furious. "What did you do?" he demanded of Max. "You didn't turn it off. What did you do?"

Max shrugged as he dragged his aching body to its feet. "Not much," he said. "I just switched the feed from your recording to…a live show."

"What live show?" Kade snapped, coming back towards Max.

Max held out his hands and grinned. "This one, of course. And when you just admitted your guilt in setting off the bomb, and revealed your plans for world domination, well, it seems that was enough to convince the alliance that maybe they were fighting the wrong people."

Kade stared at the screen and took a step back, then forward again, clearly uncertain what to do.

"It's over," Max said. "There's no way out this time."

The grumble of collapsing rock grew louder by the second, and Max imagined the Aquoran battle fleet smashing its way into the base. On the monitor, he could see screen after screen go blank as the base's cameras were knocked out. Kade cycled through more cameras and stopped at a view from inside one of the tunnels. A troop of Merryn warriors came racing down it, riding dolphins. They shot past the camera, heading into the labyrinth.

"They'll be here soon enough," Max said. "There's still time to give yourself up."

But instead Kade snatched up his oxygen face-mask, a clear visor that fitted over his skull-tight helmet.

"Don't do it, Kade," Max warned.

There was a huge explosion from above. Max looked up and saw the roof of the cavern had burst open. Aquoran subs came flooding through as rocks from the roof tumbled lazily down through the hazy water.

They're going to hit the dome! A surge of adrenaline got Max moving and he ran and dived for Lia, covering her limp body with his as the rocks smashed into the glass. Lia stirred under him.

"What's going on?" she asked, clearly still dazed.

"Hold tight!" Max told her. "This might get rough." Max shut his eyes and listened to the sound of the thick glass crunching and shattering under the heavy rocks. Tons of seawater, debris and broken shards of glass pounded down over Max. A large rock smashed painfully into his shoulder. The ground shuddered with the power of the implosion and Max clung tightly to Lia as a surge of water swept them across the floor of the dome, where they came to rest against a section of dome wall that had survived.

As the dome filled with water, Max raised his head and peered through the murky current to see that Kade was still moving. The Gustadian fitted his oxygen mask and swam quickly through the churning water towards the aquabike Max had spotted earlier. He pulled himself onto it and shot off towards the hole in the roof of the dome.

With a gasp, Max saw that as Kade was exiting the dome, something else was entering. "Tear them to pieces," Kade snarled at Loosejaw as he passed the Robobeast.

Lia's eyes widened as the giant fish raced towards them. Max saw its torpedoes arming themselves, the delivery systems moving them into position, ready to unleash the murderous weaponry. Loosejaw opened its great jaws. There was no way to escape this time – no tunnel to dart into, no passage to hide in. Max's hand found Lia's and squeezed tight.

On came Loosejaw. One of the torpedoes released and rocketed towards them, leaving a fizzing path of turbulence behind. Loosejaw banked away to the right and slowed, as if it wanted to watch the deadly missile travel all the way to its target.

And then a silver streak darted into view and intercepted the speeding missile, knocking it sideways.

"Spike!" Lia cried, as the torpedo swerved

and shot off to the left, exploding against a collapsed pile of rocks. The swordfish came whizzing towards them, into his mistress's arms. Lia clutched him in delight.

Max blinked in surprise. "He must have come in with the Merryn warriors!" he said. He looked up, expecting to see Loosejaw coming for them again.

But no. The giant fish floated, unmoving, twenty yards away where it had stopped after firing the torpedo. It was completely still, as if it had been stunned by its own light. *Why isn't it attacking?*

"I can sense something," Lia said, touching her fingers to her forehead. "There's so much Aqua Power in the cavern."

"What do you mean?" Max asked, confused.

"My people – they're stopping Loosejaw," Lia said. "They're saving us."

Max felt breathless with awe as he watched the huge fish drifting harmlessly in the gentle current within the broken dome. "I knew your Aqua Powers were strong, but…"

"Actually, I'm not sure how long they can hold it," Lia said, slightly anxious.

"My turn then!" Max said. He snatched up Kade's axe and swam quickly to the giant fish, swallowing nervously as he approached those wicked, strangely constructed jaws. Then he used the blade of the axe to prise off the blinking red light, taking care not to look at it directly.

As soon as the creature was freed from the stone, it tossed its head and swam off through the broken roof of the dome, up towards the opening in the cavern roof. As it swam, its robotic attachments fell away, piece by piece, and dropped down to the cavern floor.

"It's heading back to the temple," Lia said. "Suddenly it doesn't look quite so fearsome, does it?"

Max wanted to go and check on Rivet, but he was delayed by the arrival of a pair of Merryn warriors riding sharks. Between them they dragged the huddled figure of Kade, his armour battered and scorched.

"We caught him," they cried triumphantly. Max was about to congratulate the warriors when an Aquoran naval officer raced up on an aquabike, with a passenger sitting beside him. Lia gasped as the bike pulled up.

"We've got Kade!" the officer said. The passenger looked up. It was Kade!

"But we caught Kade," one of the Merryn said. "Look!"

"Two Kades?" Max said. A heavy feeling suddenly swelled in the pit of his stomach. "I think I might know what's going on here. Lia, is the master watch still functioning?" Lia checked the device and tapped a few keys.

"I'm removing all holograms in the local area," she said. With a flicker and a snap, both Kades suddenly changed in appearance to reveal two scowling Gustadian minions.

"Looks like he's escaped again!" Max said, slamming a fist into his palm.

Lia hung her head. "And he took my mother's ring with him."

CHAPTER NINE

THE ARCH OF PEACE

Max and Lia glided solemnly under the Arch of Peace in Sumara, following the leaders and officials of the five members of the Delta Quadrant Alliance. Max saw the Verdulan chief, Naybor, as well as the tall and coldly beautiful Empress of Arctiria. There too was General Phero of Gustados, grim and serious. And behind them were Councillor Glenon and Max's father, Callum of Aquora. The Merryn contingent waited to one side, in glittering robes.

A band played and cheering crowds lined the square, watching as King Salinus inscribed his name into a tablet. Sumara had officially become the fifth member of the alliance.

"Happy, Max," barked Rivet, racing up behind them.

Max hugged the dogbot. He'd worried that Rivet had been permanently damaged by the blow from Kade's axe. But with a recharge, a reboot and some metal work, the robodog had been restored to full functionality.

Or full health, as Lia had put it. "He's not a machine," she'd said. "He's Rivet."

Spike whizzed by overhead, performing a perfect barrel roll.

Max smiled, reflecting on the events of the last few weeks. The leaders of the five peoples had faced a hard job getting everyone to this point. Though it was clear now that Kade had been behind all the trouble, there were still bad feelings to overcome. The Verdulans didn't have the technology to pick up Kade's signal, and because they didn't see his "confession" in the lair, they were still suspicious. It took a lot of talking and expensive gifts to get them back to the negotiating table.

The Sumarans and Aquorans had come to blows outside Kade's base. There were apologies to be made and compensation paid. No one trusted the Gustadians after what Kade had done. The Arctirians refused to talk to them for weeks after the truth came out.

But eventually all agreed they were better working together than at one another's throats. The alliance was re-formed, and Sumara was once again invited to join.

Max realised he was standing next to the stern General Phero. He smiled at the Gustadian leader and bowed in respect. The general bowed back, even more deeply.

"Gustados owes you a great debt," the general said.

"What will happen to Kade's supporters?" Max asked.

"The leaders have been arrested and imprisoned," the general replied. "But most of his supporters were ordinary people terrified by his proclamations that Gustados was under threat. They were convinced that the only way to protect their families was to follow him. They were misled and have been pardoned."

"I'm glad to hear it, sir," Max said. "Kade's illusions fooled many – not just in Gustados."

There was no time to talk further – the ceremony was reaching its finale. Max, General Phero and the other dignitaries were ushered to their seats by a Merryn official. Max gazed over the plaza, ringed with onlookers from all the alliance members, lit by the glow from the palace behind. King Salinus put down his stylus and swam over to a raised lectern.

As the king waited for the crowd to hush, Max felt a glow of relief and contentment wash over him. Then Salinus began to speak.

"Fellow alliance members—" the king began. But that was all he managed to say before the crowd interrupted with a rousing cheer. "Fellow alliance members," he said again when the noise had died down. "The Delta Quadrant has long been a region of conflict and misunderstanding. For a thousand years our peoples have argued and fought. Well, I say that time has passed! I say the next thousand will not be years of strife and disagreement, but of understanding and cooperation. Let us respect our differences and celebrate them. Let us end a thousand years of war and usher in a thousand years of peace."

There was a roar of approval from the

crowd. Max rose along with everyone else, cheering, whistling and clapping.

"There are many people we need to give thanks to for delivering this peace," King Salinus went on. "The wise leaders of the alliance members who resisted war when it seemed inevitable. The diplomats who worked so hard to bring us here today. The warriors who stood firm against threats, some of whom lost their lives. But there are two people who deserve special mention – two brave souls who risked their lives again and again to stop war from blighting our land. People of Nemos, please pay your respects to Max of Aquora, and to my very own daughter, Lia of Sumara!"

Max grinned at Lia as the crowd erupted even louder than before. Lia held up a hand and Max gave her a high-five, followed by a hug. He found himself pushed forwards, towards the lectern where King Salinus waited with two gold medals.

"Well done, Max," King Salinus said, bending to pin the medal to Max's deepsuit. He then turned to Lia and pinned a second medal onto her collar before enveloping her in a huge bear hug.

"Don't forget Rivet," Max said. "Or Spike. Without them we wouldn't be here today."

Rivet raced up at the sound of his name, barking joyfully and performing a back flip. Spike whizzed overhead and raced around the perimeter of the crowd, sending the onlookers wild with excitement.

Max turned to Lia and saw tears in her eyes. "Are you OK?" he asked.

"I wish my mother was here to see this," she replied.

"She'd be so proud of you," Max said.

"But what about Kade?" Lia said. "He

escaped. And he still has her ring. I can't let him get away with it."

Max nodded. "At least with the stones locked away in your father's vaults, he can't reawaken the creatures of Deepholm." A Merryn scout had reported the guardians returned to stasis. But Max understood Lia hating the thought of her mother's ring still in Kade's possession.

Max dropped to a knee and put his arm around Rivet. He looked at his proud father clapping furiously in the crowd, then gazed up at the Arch of Peace above them. No one knew what dangers might befall the alliance in the future. But together, he and Lia would face up to any threat.

THE END

Don't miss Max's next Sea Quest adventure,
when he faces

HYDROR
THE OCEAN HUNTER

978 1 40834 097 4

WIN AN EXCLUSIVE GOODY BAG

In every Sea Quest book the Sea Quest logo is hidden in one of the pictures. Find the logo in this book, make a note of which page it appears on and go online to enter the competition at

www.seaquestbooks.co.uk

We will be picking five lucky winners to win some special Sea Quest goodies.

You can also send your entry on a postcard to:

Sea Quest Competition,
Orchard Books, Carmelite House
50 Victoria Embankment
London EC4Y 0DZ

Don't forget to include your name and address!

GOOD LUCK

Closing Date: 31st October 2016

IF YOU LIKE SEA QUEST, YOU'LL LOVE BEAST QUEST!

Series 1: COLLECT THEM ALL!

An evil wizard has enchanted the magical beasts of Avantia. Only a true hero can free the beasts and save the land. Is Tom the hero Avantia has been waiting for?

FERNO
THE FIRE DRAGON

978 1 84616 483 5

SEPRON
THE SEA SERPENT

978 1 84616 482 8

ARCTA
THE MOUNTAIN GIANT

978 1 84616 484 2

TAGUS
THE HORSE-MAN

978 1 84616 486 6

NANOOK
THE SNOW MONSTER

978 1 84616 485 9

EPOS
THE FLAME BIRD

978 1 84616 487 3

DON'T MISS THE
BRAND NEW SERIES OF:

Series 17: THE BROKEN STAR

GRYPH
THE FEATHERED FIEND

978 1 40834 076 9

THORON
THE LIVING STORM

978 1 40834 080 6

OKKO
THE SAND MONSTER

978 1 40834 082 0

SAUREX
THE SILENT CREEPER

978 1 40834 084 4

COMING SOON